THE ART OF BEING A SUPER YOU
(YOUTH EDITION)

Stan Pearson II, MBA
www.stanpearson.com

Copyright © 2019 Stan Pearson II, MBA
All rights reserved.

THE ART OF BEING A SUPER YOU

MOTIVATE AND INSPIRE OTHERS!

BOOK ME TO SPEAK

AT YOUR CONFERENCE, SCHOOL ASSEMBLY, CLASSROOM EMPOWERMENT SESSION, RETREAT OR STUDENT COUNCIL MEETING

WWW.STANPEARSON.COM

PURCHASE THIS BOOK FOR A FRIEND

SPECIAL QUANTITY DISCOUNTS

5- 20 Books	$13.97
21-99 Books	$12.97
100-499 Books	$11.97
500-999 Books	$10.97
1000+ Books	$9.97

TO PLACE AN ORDER CONTACT:
888.498.7826
STANPEARSONII@GMAIL.COM

REGISTER FOR <u>THE CLASS ACADEMY</u>, AN ONLINE LEARNING INSTITUTE THAT TEACHES CONFIDENCE, LEADERSHIP, LIFE & SOCIAL SKILLS @ WWW.CLASSACADEMYONLINE.COM

#CLASSACADEMYONLINE

DEDICATION

WOW!

Where does my dedication begin? I'm always thankful that my parents made me! (haha) I dedicate all of my growth and accomplishments to them because they quite literally made it all possible. I am also happy to mention my wife, Cynthia Padilla Pearson inspires me, loves me, respects me, and pushes me. She is a big reason why I've decided to put these thoughts to paper. Sometimes, I undervalue my ability or impact, but she's always here to remind me as I remind others that I'm better than I think I am. I dedicate this to her because she inspires me to be a better person, and because she's dedicated so much to me already in addition to bringing our incredible baby boy into the world, Stan III. Lastly, this book is dedicated to every young person who is trying to find themselves, better themselves or just aren't sure where they are or who they're suppose to be. It's okay. Life can be complex, confusing, frustrating, exciting, fun and most importantly, WORTH LIVING. I am ultimately dedicated to you. It's a process that I'll help you walk through. **Let's GOOOOOOO!**

FOREWORD: BY NOEL RODRIGUEZ

Why be yourself?

Know that as you grow, you will evolve, but do not confuse that with losing yourself, you're all you got! The person I am today is….the same person I was 20 years ago, the name is the same, same height, thank God, my culture and my ethnicity is the same.

However, how I think is different, at 47 I have evolved into a better me, why? Because I allowed myself to evolve and that makes me feel good about who I am. What has changed? I listen. I no longer feel the need to be right, and that makes me feel good because there's less weight on my shoulders. I say what's on my mind BUT with tact. That means my response factors in what I took from listening to others. I am respectful and I am more honest with people. Some might confuse that with being "blunt" or "real" but the truth is that I am ok with my truths and that settles me into a comfortable zone and I love that about myself.

The question to ask yourself is are you "real" because you feel you have something to prove or are you "real" because you no longer have anything to prove? Are you comfortable in your own skin? The key to being yourself is having a core set of fundamentals and being comfortable with being yourself in that "zone" is definitely one of them. If you are "real" because you have nothing to prove, your core will be stronger, your disagreements with others will be easier to manage, your rebuttals will be done with ease, smooth and full of confidence. Be kind, be patient and be yourself because it's a process that all of us go through.

CONTENTS

	Acknowledgments
	Foreword by Noel Rodriguez
1	Tap Into Your Spidey Senses
2	Gauge Your Inner Inner Iron Man
3	Guard Your Galaxy
4	Respect Your Time Stone
5	Pace Your Flash
6	Be Vibranium
7	You're Good You're Great You're Worth It The Truth You Tell Yourself

ACKNOWLEDGMENTS

I would like to acknowledge the students, staff & professionals I have come in contact with while on tour through 45 states in the U.S in addition to Mexico, Spain, Canada, The U.S Virgin Islands & the British Virgin Islands, Canada and other parts of the world. Every person I meet inspires me to continue my journey in life as imperfectly perfect as it is. I know I am not alone. I want to acknowledge PEOPLE, yes you. I see you. What world could we have if we saw one another more frequently and treated each other the way we'd love to be treated in our perfect world. I would also like to acknowledge the people responsible for bringing me to this point in my life; my loving wife, Cynthia Padilla Pearson, my first born,
Stanley David-Manuel Pearson III, my parents, Stanley and Patricia Pearson who remind me that when the dream is big enough, that "facts" don't count and your effort will often reflect the outcome. Care enough about yourself to see yourself, acknowledge yourself, and watch your spirit and surroundings take notice.

1 - TAP INTO YOUR SPIDEY SENSES

So, how old are you now? It's fine, you can still pause, look in the air for the answer and come up with the age that you already knew. It's what we do. We think, we learn, we grow. You might be 8 years old and reading this or you might be 18 years old reading this and still asking yourself the same questions. Who am I? What do I want to be? Who do I want to be? You might even ask yourself questions like; why don't they like me, why do they bully me or why don't I like myself? Those are pretty intense questions to start out in a book, but that's also why this book is awesome and why you'll discover even more awesomeness in yourself when you finish it or maybe even before you finish. Why do you need to tap into your Spidey Senses? That's a great question and I'm glad you asked. I wondered the same thing in grade school. I was a pretty good kid for the most part. I mean from what I remember I was a good kid. I didn't purposely hurt anyone's feelings, I was friends with most people or I thought I was, and I did my best to just get along. That doesn't always stop people from disliking you and it certainly doesn't stop you from being insecure or thinking something is wrong with you. I still had people on the bus who didn't like me very much or guys who had something to say to me as soon as I got off the bus. Some people wonder if I had a rough upbringing, did I experience extreme poverty or get abused. That isn't my truth. That wasn't my experience, but I do know I made friends who had those experiences and shared some of the same feelings I had. They too felt alone at times, insecure, bullied or weird in their own skin. Even in elementary school I sometimes felt like no matter what I did, I just didn't have what it took to fit in the way I wanted to. I noticed little by little though that the more I got to know who I was on the inside the better I felt about myself regardless of who liked or didn't like me. I had to tap into my Spidey Senses. What are those?! We all have feelings, we all have a sixth sense. We know right from wrong. We know what feels good and what doesn't. We know what makes us happy too. Tapping into your Spidey Senses means knowing what is authentic about you. It means knowing what is a part of you. If you are a Spider-man fan, think about this with me. Peter Parker was a smart kid, he was kind to people and even had a crush on someone. That didn't stop people from picking on him at times. Even though, he was smart, kind, loved by family and had a talent; he lacked the confidence to be the best version of himself. Spoiler alert, once he was bit by the spider and received his powers his confidence kicked in

IMMEDIATELY. I believe that happened in part because his new skills were far more superior than he believed himself to be, and because they were clearly more pronounced as he learned of his powers. Ask yourself what he did; I'll tell you. He practiced them day in and day out until he was more comfortable with them. He practiced them until he was more in control of them. He focused on his ability and everything that he could do. Is it at all possible that he could have done the same thing as Peter Parker before he received the bite from the spider? ABSOLUTELY! He's a great kid either way and so are you. I just want you to understand that there is so much more to you once you decide to tap into your Spidey Senses. Pay attention to the best things about you. Work on the skills you already have every day. You'll quickly realize the better you get at embracing yourself, the more you'll begin to see your confidence grow. There are unique things about you that you should pay attention to that make you who you are. Quite honestly, in plane words instead of using your "_____", I'll say Be Creative. To be creative is to be your authentic self. Use the talents and skills you were given and that you'd like to develop. Yes, you DO have a skill or a talent. Be creative in the way you move through your day. Give leftover smiles, hold a door open for someone, discard something around the house or your school that was dropped by someone else. No, it isn't yours, but it's in your presence. Being creative means doing things that everyone else might not do. Take a chance on being you. If you see a student standing outside of a classroom or event that looks lost, invite them in with a wave and a smile if you can manage a smile. Small things can make a dramatic difference when it comes to tapping into your senses also known as –being creative. You have what it takes, you just have to remember that piece and practice daily just as Peter Parker did when he realized who he had become.

"3 THINGS YOU PICKED UP"

I. USE YOUR SPIDEY SENSES
II. BE CREATIVE
III. GIVE LEFTOVER SMILES

BRAIN WORK:

USE THE FOLLOWING PAGES TO TAKE NOTES

WRITE YOUR THOUGHTS & GAME PLAN

_____
_____
_____
_____
_____
_____
_____
_____

Stan Pearson II, MBA

The Art of Being a Super You

_____
_____
_____
_____
_____
_____
_____
_____
_____
_____
_____
_____
_____
_____
_____
_____
_____

Stan Pearson II, MBA

The Art of Being a Super You

2 - GAUGE YOUR INNER IRON MAN

I LOVE IRON MAN! Ok, let me relax. Love is a strong word. I do admire Iron Man because he is brave, well thought out and he goes into all battles believing he can win them. Would that be a great way to be, live and attack your personal world? He has everything you could ever want. He has influence, confidence, MONEY, a special someone, cool friends, cool cars and is constantly developing. It's pretty awesome to think, he is a human with SUPER COOL body armor. That's the part I'd like to expound on. Iron Man is who? He's Tony Stark. Who is Tony Stark? Tony is the man, the human behind all of the cool bells and whistles. No matter how cool and indestructible he is IN the suit, he lives outside of the suit. As a matter of fact,

Tony's lifeline is attached to a machine that keeps him going. You see, sometimes we are hurting and no one can see it. Sometimes people are COOL on the outside but hurting on the inside. You'll realize if you've ever seen any of the movies that he thinks when he's Iron Man and when he's Tony Stark, but he thinks the most when he is outside of himself being who he is at the core of himself. When I tell you to gauge your inner Iron Man, I'm saying go below your surface. Have the

conversations that everyone doesn't hear. Talk about those things that everyone doesn't talk about. These self talks might be difficult but they are the ones that will help you grow the most. Know who you are at the very core of who you are daily. Ultimately, I am asking you to be your own best friend. One more time in case you didn't catch that. **Be Your Own Best Friend**. Know yourself better than anyone else knows you. I truly believe you end up in less compromising situations when you are your own best friend. That means you don't have to wait for other people to have a good time. You can have a good time, laugh, dance, talk or whatever regardless of who is around. You deserve that kind of life. Your happiness shouldn't be dependent on who told you should be enjoying yourself or not. Laugh, be kind and enjoy life all by yourself if you have to! If I'm going to be honest with you, there were times I just wanted people my age or the people I hung out with to think I was cool. Heck, I was! I was fun, kind and even athletic for the most part, so why wouldn't people like me? Unfortunately, every once in a while I did what the "cool" kids were doing so they would "see" me as cool. If they laughed at something; I would laugh even if I didn't think it was funny. If they walked a certain way, I wanted to walk that way. If they had certain clothes, I wanted to have those clothes. None of those things made me feel better. When I did them, I would end up feeling worse, because it wasn't who I was. Let me be really honest with you right now. When I was 13, I went through this stage where I REALLY

wanted my ears pierced. I just had to because so many guys in my junior high were getting their ears pierced. I mean, if it made them cool, it would DEFINITELY make me cool. I came home a few times and asked my dad. I'd say "Hey Dad, well, I think it'd be a great idea for me to get my ears pierced. Everyone is getting their ears pierced." He would kindly ignore me. (hahaha) The next year, I was 14, earrings were old news. What was next?

It was tattoos. If I was going to have a chance at finally being one of the cool guys, I'd have to get a tattoo. I wasn't always comfortable talking to my dad or asking him things, especially if they were difficult questions but this time I was ready. As he got ready for work at about 5am, I asked him a question but it was the answer that changed my life yet again. "Dad, I know I've been asking for an earring for over a year now, but I don't want an earring anymore. I'd really like a tattoo!" My dad paused which he does so very well with the poise of Denzel Washington or Thor in your favorite Denzel Washington or Thor movie, and returned with the deepest question I'd ever heard. "Son, do you think you're perfect on the inside?" No Dad, not yet. "Well, son when you think you're perfect on the inside, that's when we'll worry about changing the outside." My mind was blown. For a number of years, I was trying to change things about myself that didn't need to be changed. I wanted to change something physically in hopes that it would elevate me emotionally and intellectually. I hoped that an earring or tattoo would make me a better, more confident person. It was in that moment that I realized that no matter what I did, if I didn't work on myself from the inside, nothing I changed on the outside would ever work. If at some point those things are for you, COOL; however, I just hope and pray that you understand your value before you give "a thing" the power to tell you how amazing you are. You determine what cool is. I wanted earrings and tattoos for the wrong reason, much like you might want clothes, shoes or whatever. Those things are not what make you who you are. Be your own best friend. Gauge your inner Tony Stark. Know who you are and embrace it. The right people will want to be around you. You will find yourself being exactly where you are suppose to be and being a better version of yourself every single day. Everyone may not see your pain but it exists. You are not alone in your pain and frustration. Just know you have the tools to overcome them and reading books like this will help you overcome issues that much easier. You got this. It takes practice and persistence to get to know yourself, but you deserve it. Ask for help from family or good friends or suggestions on how to get to know yourself better. Be willing to take suggestions and possibly criticism. All of it will make you better! Thank me later!

"3 THINGS YOU PICKED UP"

I. KNOW YOUR INNER SELF
II. BE YOUR OWN BEST FRIEND
III. YOU DETERMINE WHAT COOL IS

BRAIN WORK:
USE THE FOLLOWING PAGES TO TAKE NOTES

WRITE YOUR THOUGHTS & GAME PLAN

_____
_____
_____
_____
_____
_____
_____

Stan Pearson II, MBA

The Art of Being a Super You

Stan Pearson II, MBA

The Art of Being a Super You

3 - GUARD YOUR GALAXY

I AM GROOT! I'm sorry, I just had to say that! The end. Be kind to your mind. I mean this section could end right now after that sentence, but I'd like to give you a little more content to support the notion of how important it is to guard your galaxy! Being kind to your mind is the first step. The second and overall push has to be staying in control of what you can stay in control of. You might not realize how much you are in control of, so let me give you a few examples of what you can control. Often when I think of ways to guard your galaxy I think of being present. When you decide to be present, you decide to be in the moment. You take yourself off of auto-pilot. You can control who you decide to spend time with on a regular basis. Keep in mind that no one is perfect, so its not fair to expect them to be. Heck, you aren't perfect so that's perfectly fine. However, if there is someone who isn't kind to you or who

regularly hurts your feelings without thinking about how it might affect you, you may want to consider spending less time with them. It is scientifically proven that we are affected by the people around us. That means if we are around people who make us feel bad, we will begin to feel bad all by ourselves. You are in control of these things. More importantly, let your parents, guardians, or older siblings know if there is someone around you who makes you uncomfortable or who makes you feel less than you'd like to feel. They are there to keep you safe regardless of what you think or feel. They are on your side. Have you thought about some other places in your life where you have control? You have to talk about safe places even at home. You can chat with your parents about where good places at home would be. They may be upset with me but I'd advise your parents to have a "you keep the door open policy" or at least unlocked. It would be a great idea for them to have something like that in place for you too, so you all can talk about your day. Another major place where you have control is on social media. Again, _____ Your Galaxy. Keep your mind safe. Social media is an incredible tool. It's a place where you can meet a lot of people, learn a lot of information, and create your own brand; however, it's also a place where you can run into a lot of negative information. Use social media as a positive tool. I'm going to give you some helpful to do's while on social media whether it's on YouTube, Facebook, Instagram, Twitter or Snapchat. These are general points that will typically work across the board. Quite

honestly, I dedicate 15-30 minutes of positive content per day! That's a non-negotiable.

YouTube usually helps me with this. I will just search, "motivational videos", "you can do it" or "motivate me". Any phrase like that will guide you to a video that will help you get to the right mind space. You can start off every morning with a positive YouTube video. It literally changes how you approach your day. Meditating is also helpful. Take 3 to 5 to 15 seconds to breathe in and out. It will calm you. You can even do this when you prepare for bed. If I ever have trouble sleeping or just want to fall asleep in a rested state, I repeat over and over, (peace, love, health, wealth, and happiness). I literally just say that over and over again. The next thing I know, I'm waking up! It's truly amazing, try it. It helps because those are things that I want, need and wish for daily. If you don't have a short list of things, please feel free to use mine, (peace, love, health, wealth, and happiness). I promise it works! I also created a playlist of upbeat good music. I have a playlist that literally says Upbeat Playlist. You can see in the image, I

name all of my playlists something. I do my best to be intentional about the way I feel. I don't listen to everything all of the time, but sometimes I want to guide myself. I want to guard my galaxy. I listen to all types of music for all types of reason. I'm in control of it. The other things I will do regularly is search positive #hashtags. I unfollow or unfriend negativity without feeling bad. You may feel guilty initially, but if you want to stay in a positive mind state and have control of your super powers, you have to keep your mind as clear as possible. If someone is constantly mean or rude, I distance myself from them. If they ask why, I politely let them know I'm working on some things right now and being in unhealthy environments doesn't help me get to where I want to be. They will either understand it or they won't. Most people will understand eventually whether they admit to it or not. I'll say this as I normally do, social media is an incredible tool, but if you're only using social media to be social, you're missing out. Give yourself social media time and give it a rest as well. Unfortunately, too many people associate their value with how many likes they wake up to in the morning. That isn't healthy or fair to yourself. Be kind to your mind, be good to yourself. Guard _____ _____!

Stan Pearson II, MBA

"3 THINGS YOU PICKED UP"

I. GUARD YOUR GALAXY
II. 15-30 MIN/DAY ON POSITIVE CONTENT
III. BE PRESENT

BRAIN WORK:
USE THE FOLLOWING PAGES TO TAKE NOTES

WRITE YOUR THOUGHTS & GAME PLAN

_____
_____
_____
_____
_____
_____
_____
_____

The Art of Being a Super You

The Art of Being a Super You

Stan Pearson II, MBA

4 - RESPECT YOUR TIME STONE

Time is the one thing you can't get back. You can spend money and get some more. Your parents can give you money and sometimes it seems like there's more where that came from. Maybe you have no money at all. Maybe you have to work for everything you get, so you get a job and at least if you work, you get paid. That all seems pretty fair right. Almost everything you use in your life comes back to you except for the one thing you'll wish you had more of. That one thing is time. How amazing would it be to control time or get a little time back. If you are around your parents, an older sibling, or family member go ask them right now if they ever wish they could be younger or go back in time. Most people will take a deep sigh and say, 'oh my gosh yes! No matter what they say or do after you ask them, most people will pause which means they've thought about it! (haha) You'll hear this quote more when you're older if you haven't already heard it. "Time waits for no man!" It absolutely doesn't wait for anyone. That's why you must respect time. As a young person reading this, time may not be that important to you, but pay attention to it. Enjoy your time with family and friends. Laugh a lot, dance a lot, sing a lot no matter who you think is watching. There is a time and a place for everything. I'm not saying sing and dance during class when it's inappropriate, I'm saying when the time or event presents itself, do all of the above. Sometimes we turn down our good time because we think someone is going to judge us or talk about us. Let them! They will either join in or miss out. Having the ability to respect time is an amazing super power to have. It means you don't waste it. That means you'll have to be consistent. Being consistent means finding your daily rhythm. Find a way to admire time, so it's more kind to you. When I set my alarm clock, I set it to music I love! Set a smart alarm clock. What does that mean?! Before I explain, I'll ask you one more question. Why would you set your alarm to an annoying buzzer or sound? Step your game up! Set it to your favorite song, so when you wake up, you feel good about the day. Your breath may be fire, but the song you're listening to as you start your day will be FIRE TOO! I start just about every day the same way. You should try it. I may use the restroom first, but I'll drink a cup of water, then I'll head back to my room and do 10-25 jumping jacks, 10-25 sit-ups, 10-25 pushups and run in place for like 10-15 seconds. This is not an olympic workout routine by any stretch, BUT it gets my blood going and It wakes me up. All of this is happening while I'm listening to music that I enjoy. Do you think that helps me start my day off on the right foot? It does! It takes practice so be patient. Start out light. Maybe you do 5 of everything. Just do something and remember progress over perfection. This is your rhythm for the day. Be c_____ and watch how you make the most of your time. There's no way to slow time down, but when you respect your _____ _____, you know you are doing the best with what you have. You are enjoying moments and people. When you realize how precious time is, you don't allow insignificant things to consume you. You will experience some tough times along the way, but you will move through them and not give an excess of unnecessary energy to the wrong thing. Be the same you all of the time. People shouldn't have to guess who you'll be depending on the day. Think about how you spend time with others and how you feel when you're around others. When it feels good, it's kind, it's fair, it's natural and when it isn't, you can discuss your rhythm so we continue our best efforts at respecting our time stone.

"3 THINGS YOU PICKED UP"

I. RESPECT YOUR TIME STONE
II. DO WAKE UP ACTIVITIES DAILY
III. SET A SMART ALARM CLOCK

BRAIN WORK:
USE THE FOLLOWING PAGES TO TAKE NOTES

WRITE YOUR THOUGHTS & GAME PLAN

_____
_____
_____
_____
_____
_____
_____
_____
_____

The Art of Being a Super You

Stan Pearson II, MBA

The Art of Being a Super You

Stan Pearson II, MBA

5 - PACE YOUR FLASH

I may or may not sound like someone old when I say, this is a marathon, not a sprint. We all evolve and grow at different rates. If you know Flash, it always seems like it's GO GO GO, but it isn't. Even with all of his speed, he doesn't turn it on all of the time. He understands the importance of pacing himself. I make sure I remind people often. The only person you are in competition with is the person you were yesterday. Sometimes, we look to our right or our left and wonder why we aren't going faster. Sometimes, you look behind you and think someone is gaining on you. Their race is their race. You have different goals, dreams, thoughts, abilities and heck even struggles. I wasn't always the tallest. Well, I'm STILL not the tallest, but there were plenty of times where I looked around at other guys and even other girls wishing I could just be around their height. I didn't know if people were looking at me funny or not. I knew I was looking at myself funny sometimes, even though I never told anyone. My parents would just whisper to me, "your time will come". Once that was in my head, I decided I wasn't going to worry myself. Then it started to happen! I started to grow. I stayed involved and focused and it became less important to me, because I wasn't worried about what other people were doing or how much everyone else was growing. It was cool if they did and cool if I didn't because I was pacing my flash! BOOM! It didn't matter how tall I was, I felt good being me. I was right on pace. I was running my own race at my own speed. Things don't have to happen fast. They happen when they are suppose to. If you are working hard and doing your best, just put your head down, keep being kind and it will come. It may seem like it's coming out of nowhere, but your pace has it arriving exactly when it was suppose to. It's understandable to look around a bit at what's happening around you, but don't get so caught up in it that you start to look at yourself as less of a person. You're dynamic, fun, super, and worth being around even if you don't see it yet. Give it time; _____ your flash and watch how things begin to fall into place.

Stan Pearson II, MBA

"3 THINGS YOU PICKED UP"

I. PACE YOURSELF
II. COMPETE AGAINST YOURSELF
III. RUN YOUR OWN RACE

<u>BRAIN WORK:</u>
USE THE FOLLOWING PAGES TO TAKE NOTES
WRITE YOUR THOUGHTS & GAME PLAN

_____
_____
_____
_____
_____
_____
_____
_____
_____

The Art of Being a Super You

The Art of Being a Super You

Stan Pearson II, MBA

BONUS TIPS:

6 - BE VIBRANIUM

WAKANDA FOREVER! I'm sorry, I did it again! I love Black Panther too! If you haven't gone to see it yet, treat yourself or heck, pull it up on Netflix when you have time. What is Vibranium outside of a fictional element not found not in the periodic table. I'll tell you briefly. By definition:

Vibranium is a fictional metal appearing in American comic books published by Marvel Comics. This fictional metal is noted for its uncanny ability to leverage

thermodynamics in absorbing, storing, and releasing kinetic energy in a controlled manner.

I'll give you an example of what is made from Vibranium. Have you ever heard of Captain America? Most of you have likely seen Captain America. Quite honestly Steve Rogers' transformation into Captain America is a story all by itself. It almost seems like his soul was made from Vibranium. He didn't need any piece of anything to tell him he was special. He worked hard, he stayed the course, and always gave his best even when it wasn't easy. He stood his ground when it seemed the ground shook underneath him. He didn't have all the muscles before he became the Captain, but he had all of the spirit, respect, heart and grit to be an amazing Captain. THAT is what truly made him special. Keep that in mind as you learn and grow. Who you are on the inside will radiate on the outside. It may take a while but the right people will find you, the right people will see you and more importantly, you will see yourself. Now, back to Vibranium. Black Panther and the people of Wakanda made Captain America's shield out of

The Art of Being a Super You

Vibranium. Now, we can unpack that. What is a shield? I'll tell you by definition.

noun: **shield**; plural noun: **shields**

> a broad piece of metal or another suitable material, held by straps or a handle attached on one side, used as a protection against blows or missiles.
>
> protection, guard, defense, cover, screen, shade, safety, security, shelter, safeguard, support, bulwark, protector

You get the point. A shield is a piece of metal or another suitable material that's used as protection. Now, we can couple that with a shield that is made from Vibranium. I'll even tell you that Vibranium wouldn't be considered the strongest piece of material, but it is strong, effective, and durable. It has the ability to absorb danger & impact. It has the ability to be flexible. It has the ability to feel something but not be consumed by it. Vibranium ultimately has the ability to be resilient. The is the part where I remind you that you are exactly that! You are resilient. It's possible that you are going through something right now that seems impossible but you're absorbing it, feeling it, bending, but not breaking. You must remind yourself early and often that you are Vibranium. Remind yourself to be _____. I can remember being young and sitting on the bus with tears in my eyes. I was on the soccer field, going to block the ball and instead getting kicked in the face with the ball at top speed and falling down. I remember not doing well on tests. I remember not starting on different teams I tried out for. I remember not making some teams that I tried out for. I remember things not going my way and failing often! I remember failing when I thought I would definitely win! You want to know what I remember more than all of that disappointment. I remember bouncing back from it. I remembered that I was Vibranium. I absorbed it, I felt it, I did bend, but I did not break. Be willing to fail. Be willing to try something no matter who is watching. Be willing to give something a shot that you're not good at and learn. The more you realize how resilient you are, the more you'll go for all of the things that are meant for you. Encourage your friends and family to do the same. We all have some Vibranium in us. We all have the ability to be resilient. We just have to dig for it. If you are playing a sport and something doesn't go the way you planned, you will experience disappointment. That is very natural. I tell people if they experience disappointment or are upset after a loss, that means they care! If you lose and you don't care or losing is fun you should do something different or think about why you feel the way you do. Losing is a reminder that you can do more and winning is a sign that hard work pays off and that you can still do better. You are made up of some of the best material ever. You might be thinking yea right Stan, but it's true! You are made up of a miracle. Loses and disappointment are meant to teach you. Understand that early and often and you'll receive defeat differently. You'll understand that it's your fuel to be resilient and it FEEDS your VIBRANIUM.

Stan Pearson II, MBA

"3 THINGS YOU PICKED UP"

I. ABSORB IT, FEEL IT, BEND-DON'T BREAK
II. BE RESILIENT
III. VIBRANIUM EXISTS IN YOU

BRAIN WORK:
USE THE FOLLOWING PAGES TO TAKE NOTES

WRITE YOUR THOUGHTS & GAME PLAN

_____

_____

_____

_____

_____

_____

_____

_____

_____

_____

The Art of Being a Super You

The Art of Being a Super You

7 - YOU'RE GOOD - YOU'RE GREAT - YOU'RE WORTH IT

"THE TRUTH YOU TELL YOURSELF"

I begin and end every keynote, workshop, facilitation and event I host with the above stated. You're Good, You're Great, You're Worth it. Throughout your life journey you may hear someone try to convince you of something different. Someone may tell you that you'll never be good. Someone may try to convince you that it's too hard to be great and unfortunately, there may be a very unhappy person that comes along and tells you that you are not worth it. None of those people are correct and more importantly I want to warn you that the person telling you those things could be you. The truth you tell yourself is so very important. Be honest with yourself. As we think about the truth we tell ourselves, I think of Wonder Woman. She is so many things, but her primary superpower was discovering the truth with her lasso. Sometimes, we have to wrap ourselves within truth to become the best version of ourselves. Understand that you can be honest and kind to yourself at the same time. There's no need to call yourself dumb or stupid or whatever.

Yeap, you made a mistake. Who doesn't? If you do call yourself a bad name, put your mind in reverse and correct it with something positive. It's a small adjustment but it's worth doing. We will eventually believe what we say to ourselves. That's why the truth you tell yourself is so important. Does that make sense? Yes or No and why?

_____

_____

_____

_____

It's been great spending this time with you. I hope you have had a chance to reflect and consider some of what you've read. It would make perfect sense to read this more than once to get the principles under your belt as you have more experiences, and even pass it along to a friend or family member you think it can help. You have what it takes to be a Super You. There's no better feeling than being at peace with yourself as you discover *The Art of Being You, a Super You*. Being you is a full-time job. Why try to be anyone else? The "cool" person you see has issues and insecurities too. They may just be better at hiding them. Embrace all that is you and just commit to making yourself better every single day. You aren't supposed to make yourself perfect; you're just supposed to make progress.

"3 THINGS YOU PICKED UP"

I. _____
II. _____
III. _____
(YEAP, ON YOUR OWN THIS TIME. BUT YOU GOT IT!)

BRAIN WORK:
USE THE FOLLOWING PAGES TO TAKE NOTES

WRITE YOUR THOUGHTS & GAME PLAN

_____

_____

_____

_____

_____

_____

_____

_____

Stan Pearson II, MBA

The Art of Being a Super You

Stan Pearson II, MBA

DAILY GOALS:

1. BE CREATIVE
2. BE YOUR OWN BEST FRIEND
3. BE PRESENT
4. BE CONSISTENT
5. BE RESILIENT

RHYTHM TO DO'S:
DAILY ACTIVITIES
YES, 7 DAYS A WEEK!

SET YOUR ALARM TO SONGS YOU LIKE
START WITH ANY COMBINATION OF THE BELOW IF YOU ARE ABLE:
- 5 JUMPING JACKS
- 15 SECONDS OF MEDITATION
- 5 DEEP BREATHS
- 5 PUSH-UPS
- 5 SIT-UPS
- 5 MINUTES OF JOURNALING
- GREET EVERYONE IN THE HOUSE
- TELL YOURSELF "I LOVE YOU"
- VOICE MEMO ADDITIONAL DAILY GOALS
- SAY THANK YOU FOR ASSISTANCE OR HELP IN ANYWAY.
- APOLOGIZE WHEN YOU HURT SOMEONE'S FEELINGS
- ASK HOW YOU CAN BE BETTER
- SOCIAL MEDIA - **IF IT ISN'T POSITIVE, DON'T POST IT.** (BEFORE YOU POST ANYTHING ASK YOURSELF, "DOES THIS MAKE SENSE?")

THANK YOU FOR TAKING THIS JOURNEY WITH ME!
KNOW YOURSELF, LOVE YOURSELF, BE YOURSELF

ABOUT THE AUTHOR

Who is Stan Pearson, II? He's an outgoing, funny charismatic guy who loves his family and loves what he does. He enjoys giving people the right tools to change themselves. He was in the band in school, playing the trumpet and snare on drum line which turned into playing for one of the best high schools in the United States, Marian Catholic High School. Two Grand National Championships was something incredible to be a part of. During Stan's senior year he suffered a very scary neck injury at football practice bruising his vertebrae. Though Stan loves sports and competing, it made his decision to pursue music much easier. Well, that and the partial music scholarship to Missouri Western State University. He had his ups and downs in college while being

involved and learning so much along the way. Those ups and downs helped him to become a Governor's Staffer and Former Capitol Hill Staffer.

Present day, Stan Pearson II, is a bi-lingual Award Winning Speaker, Motivational Comedian, Consultant and event Host. His comedic style, engaging activities, and real life easy to apply expertise connect with audiences all around the world. His approach helps people open up their minds and their hearts for a true life-changing experience.

Stan has spoken in over 45 States in the U.S. in addition to Mexico, the British Virgin Islands, Spain, The U.S Virgin Islands and Canada. His presentations connect, entertain, and educate everyone regardless of race, cultural, or socio-economic backgrounds or belief system. If you are looking for a speaker or event host who is one of the best in the world while engaging, entertaining and educating your audience; look no further, Stan is your man!

YOU DESERVE THE BEST!

Stan Pearson II, MBA

Motivate and INSPIRE OTHERS!

BOOK ME TO SPEAK

AT YOUR CONFERENCE, SCHOOL ASSEMBLY, CLASSROOM EMPOWERMENT SESSION, RETREAT OR STUDENT COUNCIL MEETING

WWW.STANPEARSON.COM

PURCHASE THIS BOOK FOR A FRIEND

SPECIAL QUANTITY DISCOUNTS

5- 20 Books	$13.97
21-99 Books	$12.97
100-499 Books	$11.97
500-999 Books	$10.97
1000+ Books	$9.97

TO PLACE AN ORDER CONTACT:
888.498.7826
STANPEARSONII@GMAIL.COM

REGISTER FOR THE CLASS ACADEMY, AN ONLINE LEARNING INSTITUTE THAT TEACHES CONFIDENCE, LEADERSHIP, LIFE & SOCIAL SKILLS @ WWW.CLASSACADEMYONLINE.COM

Made in United States
North Haven, CT
12 October 2024